Under the
MAMBO MOON

Julia Durango

Illustrated by Fabricio VandenBroeck

ioi Charlesbridge

On summer nights
Papi lets me help out
at the music store.

Papi says you can
read people's souls
by the music
they listen to;
that hearts
fly home
when the music's
Just Right.

Papi says
people come here
to buy dreams
and memories.

Mrs. García
gets off at the bus stop
in front of the store.
She walks slowly,
one hand on her back,
trying to push away an ache.
She's been cleaning houses
all day,
but still she smiles
and stops to talk.

João hangs out by the door
pretending not to watch
the girls go by.
"A boy that handsome
can only be trouble,"
Mrs. García says.
João likes to talk music
with Papi.

Mrs. García

On the day of my *quinceañera*,
I wore a gown
of blushing pink
and a gold tiara.

The tiny rosebuds on my cake
matched the real ones
in my bouquet,
and my gifts reached the ceiling.

A handsome mariachi band
played all afternoon
and serenaded me with
"Las mañanitas."

On the day of my *quinceañera*,
I was in Mariachi Heaven.

Mariachi

João

A girl from Ipanema
(no one ever knew her name)
caught the eye of a composer
who would never be the same.

"She's a little bit of samba,
with a pinch of jazz thrown in.
She's the strum of my *violão*—
such a girl there's never been."

Then he wrote a brand-new song
for the girl without a name,
who strolled along the beach
and brought the bossa nova fame.

Bossa nova

Dr. Solís enters,
his white hair
sticking out all over.
"Hey, Doc Einstein!"
João calls.
Dr. Solís chuckles
and wipes his brow
with a linen handkerchief.

Catalina arrives
with mangoes
from the corner grocery.
She sneaks up
and gives Dr. Solís
a peck on the cheek.
João blushes.

Tía Pepa hurries in,
her arms full of shopping bags.
Catalina says, *"Hasta pronto,"*
and hides in the aisles.
João follows.
Even Dr. Solís makes a beeline
for the back of the store.
Tía Pepa likes to talk.

Dr. Solís

Just as the *bomba* drummers
call to each other,
challenging the dancers
to reply,
a salty Puerto Rican breeze
wends its way north
and whispers in my ear.

And just like the dancers
who answer the call,
heeding the summons
of the beating drums,
an old man becomes
young again and remembers
his island home.

Bomba

Catalina

Some people like to waltz away the evening
in tuxedos and gowns and gloves,
gliding in the moonlight
like fancy paper dolls.

But me? Not me, *mamita.*

Me, I like to slide on my party dress
and hot pink heels,
so I can shine like a jewel
on the crowded dance room floor.

And when the *charanga* starts to play,
and the guiro makes that
chee-yah-chih-chih sound—

then, *mamita,* then,
I'll dance the cha-cha-cha.
No waltzing for me—I like to

     Cha-

         Cha-

     Cha.

cha-cha-cha

Tía Pepa

Marisol!

How are you?

Ana's wedding,

much to do!

Choose the music,

something fun.

Need to please

everyone.

The merengue?

Why, that's great.

Whip things up;

I can't wait!

Can you see it?

Picture this:

Ana's wedding—

perfect bliss.

Kiss the bride,

hug the groom,

move the chairs,

clear the room,

find a partner,

start the band.

Bride and groom,

hand in hand.

Then we'll dance,

spin and sway,

'til the night

welcomes day.

Sun comes up,

take a peek.

Bride and groom,

cheek to cheek!

Merengue

Gabriel and Mila come in
to flip through CDs.
I leave Tía Pepa to Papi
and join them.
Gabriel doesn't talk much
at school, but with us,
he and his green eyes always
have something to say.

Professor Soto
speaks with Papi now,
his voice rippling
with Andean accents.
Gabriel, Mila, and I
move closer
to listen.

Mila scoops the long braids
off her neck and
pulls us aside.
"I think the professor's
missing home,"
she says with a sad smile.
"I know how he feels."

Gabriel

Tío Freddy says
his accordion is *puro colombiano*
and will only play *vallenatos*.

> "The soul of our valley,
> the poetry of our people,
> the pride of our homeland, Gabriel."

Tío Freddy says
he's saving his money
so he can take me to Colombia
someday.

> "We'll eat *buñuelos* and *bocadillos*
> and listen to *vallenato* music
> all night long, muchacho."

Mamá says
Tío Freddy is as *puro colombiano*
as his homesick accordion.

Vallenato

Professor Soto

Yesterday
the *zampoña* player
stood in the park with his *compadres,*
trying to remember where he was
after twenty-seven concerts
in five countries.

Slowly
the haunted sound
of ancient instruments
sent a shiver through the crowd,
echoing the weathered majesty
of distant Andean peaks.

I watched
the *zampoña* player
close his eyes, and I knew he was alone,
listening to the wind whistle through
the familiar cracks and crevices
of his highland home.

Andean

Mila

When my great-great-grandparents
were slaves in Uruguay,
they would beat upon their drums.
They would dance the *candombé*.

When lonely mother Africa
heard their sounds across the sea,
she sent a message back:

> *Children,*
> *please*
> *come*
> *home*
> *to*
> *me.*

Candombé

Mr. Mayer holds the door open
for Mrs. Mayer,
who looks like
an old-time movie star
with her high heels
and swept-back hair.
Papi asks them to give us
a quick tango lesson.

Samuel stops in
to show us
his new skateboard.
He says Mrs. Mayer
is a tango goddess,
and Mr. Mayer beams.
But, Samuel says,
tango isn't the only
game in town.

Mr. and Mrs. Mayer

Hair slicked back.
Heads together.
But underneath . . .

our legs
　　　　twirl and
　　　　　　　　swizzle like
　　　　a handful of
licorice whips.

Shoulders straight.
Arms in place.
But underneath . . .

　　　　our legs
　　　swivel and
turn like
　　　　an electric
　　　　　　taffy pull.

Eyes forward.
Lips closed.
But underneath . . .

our legs
　　　　laugh and
　　　　　　tell secrets
　　　　like kids in
a candy store.

Tango

Samuel

Samba school is cool, know why?
The students aim to satisfy.
We play our music every night
and practice 'til we get it right.
We sew our costumes, shine our shoes,
build a float, and learn new moves—
all for Rio's grand parade:
Carnaval, the masquerade!
And on the day of our big test,
we students do our very best
to demonstrate with charm and ease
our samba music expertise.
There's only ONE important rule—

You gotta have fun in samba school!

Samba

Susana and her neighbor Cristian
come in next, laughing at some
private joke. Susana, with her
preschool-teacher perkiness,
bubbles with enthusiasm
as she greets each
of us in turn.
"Marisol, look at you!
Almost a woman already!"

Now I'm blushing,
but Cristian quickly changes
the subject back
to music.
I smile at him gratefully,
and when he smiles in return,
I understand why all
the high-school girls
have a crush on him.

Liliana arrives
five minutes before close,
her thin shoulders slumped
under the weight of a full backpack.
She says between double shifts
and summer school
she can barely breathe,
but tonight
she and her *novio,* Rubén,
are going dancing
no matter what.

Susana

I can't listen
    to *son jarocho*
without
    dancing—
as soon as I hear
    the harp's arpeggios,
sharp and sparkling
    like cool raindrops
on a flat tin roof,
    I'm back in
Veracruz
    surrounded by
jarochos in white,
    their voices
harmonizing
    like a band of angels.
My heart skips
    around my ribcage
in 6/8 time.
    My feet can't stop
tap   tap   tapping.
    My whole body
sings.

Son jarocho

Cristian

When the Spanish noblemen
of Cartagena
heard the *cumbia* drums
at night,
they would
shake their heads,
lock their doors,
shut their windows,
afraid of vengeful
spirits let loose
with every
drumbeat.
"Sinners!"
they would cry,
while outside
their slaves
danced and
courted one
another—
celebrating
life,
remembering
love.

Cumbia

Liliana

When I salsa with Rubén,
my troubles leave me
like a flock of twitchy birds
flying south for the season.
I don't have to think;
I just follow Rubén's lead,
resting easy in the safety
of his smile.

The couples around us
move to the beat of the claves,
twirling and laughing,
just like me and Rubén—
like we're all in this together,
like the whole world
will be okay, as long as
we keep dancing.

When I salsa with Rubén,
life is sweet and *picante*
at the same time.

Salsa

One by one,
each person says,
"Adios! Ciao! Good night!"
Papi and I clean the counters
and lock up the store.

We walk home
beneath streetlights
and neon signs,
listening to
the city hum
its own melody.

Marisol

Sometimes I get to stay up late after we get home. Papi strings lights around the patio, Mami makes *limonada*, and I dust off the records. "Be careful, *m'ijita*," Papi says. "Don't scratch the family fortune." Mami laughs, gives Papi a wink, and we dance under the Mambo Moon.

Mambo

AUTHOR'S NOTE

The amazing diversity and range of Latin American music and dance reflect the mix of traditions brought to the region by three groups of people. Originally inhabited by hundreds of indigenous tribes, Latin America was conquered and claimed by Europeans (the Spaniards, Portuguese, and others), shortly after Columbus landed on its shores in 1492. These settlers soon brought millions of African slaves to work in their new mines and plantations.

The musical traditions of these three groups soon began to influence each other. Musicians wove together the sounds of indigenous flutes and scrapers (percussion instruments), European stringed instruments, and African drums. As they experimented with new musical forms and instruments, dozens of exciting rhythms emerged. Today the influence of Latin music can be heard in many types of music, including rock, pop, and hip-hop.

While I've tried to include a wide variety of music here, there are many other Latin musical traditions to explore. The best way to appreciate music, of course, is to listen to it—you can find excellent Latin music in most libraries and music stores.

And don't forget to dance!

MEXICO
CUBA
DOMINICAN REPUBLIC
PUERTO RICO
COLOMBIA
ECUADOR
PERU
BRAZIL
BOLIVIA
ARGENTINA
URUGUAY
CHILE

ABOUT THE MUSIC

Andean music is best known for the whistling sounds of the indigenous *quena* (flute) and *zampoña* (panpipes). The musicians of the central Andes adapted the Spanish guitar by making it smaller and more portable. Given the scarcity of wood in the highlands, these guitars, called *charangos,* were often crafted from armadillo shells. The central Andean countries include Ecuador, Peru, Bolivia, Argentina, and Chile.

Bomba music was brought to Puerto Rico by the African slaves who worked on the island's sugar plantations. *Bomba* drummers play two barrel-shaped drums, the larger drum "calling" to the smaller one, and both drums calling and responding to the dancers. Maracas (shakers) and sticks are played to accompany the drums.

The **bossa nova** was first heard in Brazil in the late 1950s, when composers combined the cool jazz of the United States with soft samba rhythms played on the guitar. The most famous bossa nova song is called "The Girl from Ipanema," a tune familiar around the world.

Candombé originated among the Bantu people of eastern Africa. The drum-based music was brought to Uruguay during the slave trade and is still widely performed at parties and carnivals. *Candombé* is played with drums of three different sizes.

Cha-cha-cha is a quick three-step dance inspired by the Cuban mambo. Most people know it as "the cha-cha." Mambo and cha-cha-cha music are often played by a *charanga,* an instrumental band that usually includes a piano, bass, flute, violins, timbales, and a guiro (a scraper made from a notched gourd and stick).

Cumbia is one of Colombia's most well-known folk dances and musical forms. Originally performed as a courtship ritual among African slaves, *cumbia* was primarily played with drums and claves (hard, thick sticks). Later, Amerindian flutes and guiros were added, as were European guitars and accordions.

Mambo music emerged in Cuba in the 1940s when Cuban dance bands added conga drums and brass instruments to their *charanga* groups, giving their rhythms a jazzier sound. "Mambo" is the Bantu word for "conversation with the gods."

The famous **mariachi** bands of Mexico include several violins, two trumpets, a traditional guitar, a high-pitched guitar called a *vihuela,* a deep-pitched guitar called a *guitarrón,* and a Mexican folk harp. Mariachi bands often play at parties and special events like the *quinceañera,* a celebration held on a girl's fifteenth birthday to commemorate her transition to adulthood. *"Las mañanitas"* is a popular birthday song.

Merengue is a fast-paced rhythm played by Latin dance bands that usually features horns or an accordion. Merengue is considered the national dance of the Dominican Republic, though its popularity is widespread throughout Latin America and the Caribbean.

Although **salsa** music has roots in Puerto Rico and Cuba, the term "salsa" was coined by New York Latinos, who incorporated elements of US jazz and rock into their music. Salsa encompasses many styles of music, including the mambo and cha-cha-cha, and is one of the most popular types of Latin music and dance.

From the time the African-influenced **samba** emerged in Brazil in the 1920s, the music has been closely linked with the pre-Lent celebration of *Carnaval*. Neighborhood groups of Africans in Rio de Janeiro formed to play music and parade down the streets during *Carnaval*. Still popular today, these "samba schools" meet year-round to work on their costumes, music, and dances.

Son jarocho refers to a distinctive musical style born in Veracruz, Mexico, that was strongly influenced by 17th- and 18th-century Spanish dance music. *Son jarocho* is played with stringed instruments, including several small guitars and a harp. In plural form, the word *jarochos* refers to the groups of minstrel musicians, often wearing white suits and cowboy hats, who play this music.

Tango is one of the most famous Latin dances, known for its passionate, stylized moves and walking steps. A tango orchestra usually includes a piano, violin, contrabass, *bandoneon* (a type of accordion), and sometimes a guitar. Argentina is famous for its tango musicians and dancers.

Vallenato music originated in the eastern valley region of Colombia. A traditional *vallenato* ensemble is made up of three instruments, which some say represent the mixed ancestry of Colombia: the accordion (European), the *caja* (a single-headed cylinder drum from Africa), and the *guacharaca* (an indigenous scraper).

For Katalina and Juliana, with love—J. D.

For Ian, the tiny dancer—F. V.

Text copyright © 2011 by Julia Durango
Illustrations copyright © 2011 by Fabricio VandenBroeck
All rights reserved, including the right of reproduction in whole or in part in any form.
Charlesbridge and colophon are registered trademarks of Charlesbridge Publishing, Inc.

Published by Charlesbridge
85 Main Street
Watertown, MA 02472
(617) 926-0329
www.charlesbridge.com

Library of Congress Cataloging-in-Publication Data
Durango, Julia, 1967–
    Under the mambo moon / Julia Durango ; illustrated by Fabricio VandenBroeck.
        p. cm.
    ISBN 978-1-57091-723-3 (reinforced for library use)
I. VandenBroeck, Fabricio, 1954– II. Title.
PS3604.U727U53 2010
811'.6—dc22   2008007255

Printed in China
(hc) 10 9 8 7 6 5 4 3 2 1

Illustrations done in acrylics and colored pencils on paper texturized with gesso, fine plaster,
    and titanium white
Display type and text type set in Madrid, ITC Legacy Serif, p22 Tai Chi, and TheSans
Color separations by Chroma Graphics, Singapore
Printed and bound February 2011 by Jade Productions in ShenZhen, Guangdong, China
Production supervision by Brian G. Walker
Designed by Martha MacLeod Sikkema